Dragon Dance

by Sue Graves and Fátima Anaya

FRANKLIN WATTS

LONDON•SYDNEY

Chapter 1

Ju-Long's cousin, Ting, came over to stay and they were very excited. It would soon be New Year, and everyone was getting ready to celebrate. Ju-Long's mum was busy cleaning the house.

AS394813

Libraries, Information and Archives

This item is to be returned on or before the last date shown below

SDE

0 6 NOV 2019

1 6 JUL 2022

2 7 JAN 2023

1 5 NOV 2023

2 6 JAN 2024

1 8 APR 2024

JS

Central Support Unit • Catherine Street • Dumfries • DG1 1JB
T. 01387 253820 • F. 01387 260294 • E. yourlibrary@dumgal.gov.uk

24 Hour loan renewal on our website
WWW.DUMGAL.GOV.UK/LIA

Dumfries
& Galloway

DUMFRIES & GALLOWAY LIBRARIES	
AS394813	
Askews & Holts	Jan-2019
JF	£8.99

She told the children that everyone liked to clean their homes in time for New Year.

"Just like we always do," she said.

"Why do we clean the house before New Year?" asked Ju-Long.

"It sweeps out the old year to let in the new," said Mum. "It feels like a new beginning. Ju-long, you should tidy your bedroom!"

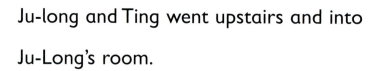

Ju-long and Ting went upstairs and into Ju-Long's room.

"What a mess," said Ting.

"I know," agreed Ju-Long. He smiled at his cousin.

"Will you help me tidy it up?"

"Okay," said Ting, "as long as you help, too."

"Of course!" said Ju-Long.

Ting started to tidy up and put things away.

But Ju-long didn't help at all. He had found

a dragon mask amongst his toys.

"Look at me!" he shouted. "I'm a scary dragon."

He danced around the room running circles
round Ting until she stopped trying to tidy up
and sat down. "Stop it!" she laughed, "I'm not
tidying up if you're not."

Chapter 2

Every New Year, the whole family went to stay

with Yeye and Nie Nie who lived in the village.

Each year, the children made gifts to take

to their grandparents.

"What shall we make for Yeye and Nie Nie

this year?" asked Dad.

"Let's make some red lanterns," said Ting.

"Good idea," said Dad. "Red is the

luckiest colour in China, after all!"

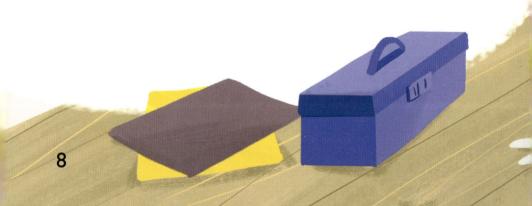

9

But Ju-Long didn't want to make a lantern.

He just wanted to dance around in

his dragon mask, pretending to be a dragon.

"I love staying with Yeye and Nie Nie,"

said Ju-Long. "The New Year parade

in their village is brilliant. I like the dragon dance

best of all. I wish I could dance in that costume.

Perhaps one day I will."

"What else do you like about New Year?"
Dad asked him.

"I like it when Yeye gives us lucky red envelopes,"
said Ju-Long. "There's always money inside."

Dad laughed. "Do you know what you want to
buy with your money this year?" he asked.

"Oh yes," said Ju-Long. "I want to buy a dragon
costume. Dragons are brilliant!"

Chapter 3

That evening they all drove to the village.

Yeye and Nie Nie were waiting for them.

Ting gave Nie Nie the red lantern.

"It's lovely," said Nie Nie. She hung it up near

the front door. "It will be sure to bring us

lots of good luck."

Soon it was time for supper. Nie Nie had made

lots of delicious things to eat.

"I think you are the best cook in the world,"

said Ju-Long happily as he filled up his bowl.

Nie Nie laughed.

When they had finished eating, Yeye stood up
and looked at Nie Nie with a smile.

"I think it's time for the lucky red envelopes,
don't you?" he said, turning to Ting and Ju-Long.

"Yes, please," shouted the children.

Yeye handed them the lucky red envelopes.

"What will you buy with your money?" he asked.

"I don't know yet," said Ting.

"I'm going to buy a dragon costume,"
said Ju-Long. "I love dragons."

"Ah, yes!" said Yeye. "We'll look out for the dragon
when we watch the parade."

Chapter 4

After supper, Yeye picked up a beautiful box and settled down by the fire. Just like he did each year, Yeye told the children stories about the New Year parades when he was a boy.

"There were lion dances, firecrackers and music," he said. "The parade went on and on. It was always wonderful. Best of all was the dragon dance. It was amazing!"

Ju-Long sighed. "I wish I could do the dragon dance," he said.

"Perhaps one day you will," said Yeye.

Yeye told them about the dragon costume.

"The dancers still use the same costume

that was used when I was a boy," he said,

showing them some photos. "I liked the way

the dragon's huge head moved and the jaws

snapped up and down. And I really loved

its big rolling red eyes."

"I like the red and yellow ribbons that look like

flames in its mouth," said Ting.

"But who's inside the costume?" asked Ju-Long,

looking puzzled.

"It's always children from the village school,"

said Yeye. He reached to the bottom of the box.

"I have something special to show you," he said.

Yeye took out another photo. It was very old.

The photo was of a large dragon.

A boy was standing by it.

"Can you guess who the boy is?" asked Yeye.

Ting and Ju-Long peered closely at the photo.

"It's you, Yeye!" cried Ting.

"Yes, it's me," laughed Yeye. "I danced lots of times

in the dragon costume. I always danced in the tail.

It was fun because I could swish it from side to side."

"I didn't know that," said Ju-Long. "I wish

I could do the dragon dance like you."

"I'm afraid only children from the village

can take part in the dance," said Yeye.

21

Chapter 5

Later, they all went to watch the parade.

Everyone from the village was out on the street.

There were flags and streamers.

There was lots of music, too.

Yeye looked at his watch.

"The parade should start very soon," he said.

Then the teacher from the village school came over to them. He looked worried.

"What's the matter, Mr Chan?" asked Yeye.

23

"It's the dragon dance," said Mr Chan. "The boy who was to be in the head of the dragon is ill. We can't do the dance today. We don't have enough children to do it properly."

Then Ting had a good idea.

"What about Ju-Long?" she said. "He could be in the dragon's head. He'd be brilliant. He's great at pretending to be a dragon!"

A few minutes later, the parade started.

There were dancers and drummers.

There were people in amazing costumes.

Last of all came the huge dragon. Ju-Long made its head swing from side to side. He snapped its jaws up and down. He twisted and turned and jumped and skipped. He made the red eyes roll. Everyone clapped and cheered and said it was the best dragon dance they had ever seen.

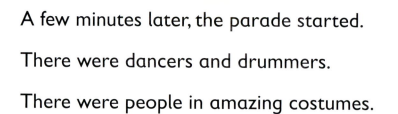

Soon the parade was over.

"You were brilliant," Mr Chan called to Ju-Long as everybody clapped and cheered. "Well done!"

Yeye gave Ju-Long a pat on the back.
"I'm not surprised you were so good at
the dragon dance," he said with a grin.
Ju-Long looked puzzled. "Why?" he asked.
"Because your name means 'as powerful as
a dragon'!" laughed Yeye.

Things to think about

1. Why does Ju-Long's mum say she is tidying the house at the start of the story?
2. Why does Ting stop helping tidy up?
3. What does their grandfather show them pictures of?
4. Why is Mr Chan worried when the family meet him before the parade?
5. Have you ever taken part in celebrating a festival? Or would you like to? Which festival do you celebrate?

Write it yourself

This story is about an important celebration.
Now write a story about a different family holding a celebration. Plan your story before you begin to write it. Start off with a story map:

• a beginning to introduce the characters and where and when your story is set (the setting);
• a problem which the main characters will need to fix in the story;
• an ending where the problems are resolved.

Get writing! Try to use interesting details about the celebration, such as the tradition of giving red envelopes of money for Chinese New Year, to describe your story world to your reader.

Notes for parents and carers

Independent reading
The aim of independent reading is to read this book with ease. This series is designed to provide an opportunity for your child to read for pleasure and enjoyment. These notes are written for you to help your child make the most of this book.

About the book
In this story, we follow Ju-Long, Ting and their family as they prepare to and then celebrate Chinese New Year. Ju-Long is not much help in cleaning the house before New Year, but he saves the day by taking part in the dragon dance at the parade.

Before reading
Ask your child why they have selected this book. Look at the title and blurb together. What do they think it will be about? Do they think they will like it?

During reading
Encourage your child to read independently. If they get stuck on a longer word, remind them that they can find syllable chunks that can be sounded out from left to right. They can also read on in the sentence and think about what would make sense.

After reading
Support comprehension by talking about the story. What happened?
Then help your child think about the messages in the book that go beyond the story, using the questions on the page opposite.
Give your child a chance to respond to the story, asking:
Did you enjoy the story and why? Who was your favourite character?
What was your favourite part? What did you expect to happen at the end?

Franklin Watts
First published in Great Britain in 2018
by The Watts Publishing Group

Copyright © The Watts Publishing Group 2018
All rights reserved.

Series Editors: Jackie Hamley and Melanie Palmer
Series Advisors: Dr Sue Bodman and Glen Franklin
Series Designer: Peter Scoulding

A CIP catalogue record for this book is
available from the British Library.

ISBN 978 1 4451 6325 3 (hbk)
ISBN 978 1 4451 6326 0 (pbk)
ISBN 978 1 4451 6324 6 (library ebook)

Printed in China

Franklin Watts
An imprint of
Hachette Children's Group
Part of The Watts Publishing Group
Carmelite House
50 Victoria Embankment
London EC4Y 0DZ

An Hachette UK Company
www.hachette.co.uk

www.franklinwatts.co.uk

FSC
www.fsc.org
MIX
Paper from
responsible sources
FSC® C104740